When the Sea Meets the River

SHIVA PRASAD MILI

Notion Press India

Old No.38, New No.6

Mc Nichols Road, Chetpet

Chennai-600031

First edition 2024

ISBN: *979-889415890-7*

Printed and bound in India by
Notion Press

Acknowledgements

In the creation of this work, I am profoundly indebted to the people and the enchanting locale of Disangmukh. As custodians of a rich heritage of tribal lore and legends, you have provided a wellspring of inspiration for my literary endeavours. The riverine beauty of Disangmukh has been a generous muse, offering ample ingredients to nourish the narrative of this novella.

A heartfelt thanks to **Durgiram Mili** and **Anuj Yein,** whose insights into the uncountable mysteries of Disangmukh have been invaluable. Your insistence on sharing these wonders with the world has been the catalyst for the retelling of this true love saga. It is through your eyes that the readers will embark on a journey of discovery, unveiling the secrets of Disangmukh to the world beyond.

Dedicated

To

The wanderers who traverse seas and rivers, unwittingly fall in love with the untouched charm of rustic damsels. This novella honours those who, in the throes of love, find themselves dismantling cultural divides.

It is also for the silent communicators of affection, *who comprehend love not as a language to be spoken, but as a feeling to be shared*. For those who know no barriers when it comes to the heart's call, may this story echo your unspoken truths.

Preface

In the verdant embrace of Assam's heartland, by the meandering Brahmaputra, lies Disangmukh—a village that is a testament to tradition and a keeper of stories. Here, in the district of Sibsagar, my story finds its roots, intertwined with the pulse of an ancient culture. My connection to this tranquil hamlet transcends mere geography; it is a bond woven through the fabric of time.

My life's journey, rich with exploration, invariably draws me back to my birthplace. Disangmukh beckons and I heed its call, returning to my origins whenever fate allows. Each visit is a pilgrimage, a return to a place where history speaks through the elders, and the veil between the seen and unseen is tantalizingly thin.

Amidst the serenity of Disangmukh, I am captivated by stories that are the lifeblood of the Mising community. These are not mere myths;

they are the living history of their people. The tales passed down through generations, are imbued with the mystical aura of the village, compelling me to document them—a chronicle of the extraordinary.

Yet, within this rich tapestry of folklore, there is one narrative that stands out—the true love story of Oikoli. Even though it is not a tale, this saga, unknown to the people of Disangukh for over a century, was revealed to me by my friends Durgiram Mili and Anuj Yein from Ligiri Bari Village. Their accounts allowed me to reframe and recreate this plot. *I hold this love saga in the same regard as the most revered folktales or legends.* As this book brings it to light, I believe our new generation will see it as a folktale that had, until now, remained unnoticed in the collective memory.

The pages that follow will take you on a journey through time and culture, exploring the profound romance and cultural engagement that unfolded in Disangmukh. The saga of Oikoli, interwoven with the Britishers' arrival and their encounter with the mystical, forms the heart of this narrative.

Contents

"What's past is Prologue."

William Shakespeare, 'The Tempest'

Prologue

Beneath the vast canvas of an azure sky, the village of Disangnmukh lies cradled in the tender arms of nature. Here, amidst the whispering reeds and the kans grass-strewn riverbanks, the seed of my story sprouted. It was not just **Probin Sharma** and **Madine Hazarika**, my propellers, but also **Dr Ananda Bormudoi,** the esteemed critic; **Prof Mridul Bordoli,** the learned academician; and **Dr Saumerjyoti Mahanta,** the scholarly writer, **Dr Protim Sharma**, a columnist and **Pranjal Protim Borah,** a prolific writer who collectively fanned the flames of my creative spirit. They bestowed upon me a mantra, **"Be Mising first, be yourself and let the world know your roots through English,"** which I've woven into the very fabric of my narrative. This dictum became the guiding principle of my writing journey.

With each return to Disangnmukh, the village's reeds and kans grass, its open fields where cattle graze, beckon me to immortalize their beauty in prose. They implore me to craft a tapestry of words that breathes life into the land, making the ephemeral, eternal.

Seven sunsets had passed when I roamed Disangnmukh's familiar trails, each footfall echoing a line of poetry from the **anthology of Homecoming**. The village, my muse, whispered promises of untold tales. As dusk draped the heavens in a cloak of fiery amber, I stumbled upon the village elders. Their visages, maps of life's intricate paths, were gathered around the hearth's warm glow, engaging in the hallowed ritual of **Apong** and pork, their stories ascending with the smoke to the stars.

In the dance of shadows, **Durgiram Mili**, a friend rooted as deeply as the ancient Mising abodes, shared a tale imbued with our land's soul. This narrative, dear reader, is a patchwork of human encounters, weaving together the bitter and the sweet, sorrows and joys.

Dear Reader,

Thank you for choosing this novel. This story will transport you to the world of tribal people by the riverbank, offering an experience unlike any other novel.

Happy Reading!

Shiva

Mising Oini:tom

"Adié kéígdo a:né korongé

Jiri Jiri:pé bidyarra dung,

A:né kéréng kéré:do

Misingé do:lungé

To:dílokké lu:yarra dung."

Meaning in English:

In the foothills, rivers of yore,
Flow like streams, evermore.
And beside these waters, clear and still,
Mising villages stand, as they always will.

Intentionally left blank

CHAPTER 1

Journey to the Core

"Nature never did betray the heart that loved her." - William Wordsworth,

(TinternAbbey)

The sun hung low on the horizon, casting a dazzling golden hue over the lush, green landscape of Disangmukh. The

village, nestled serenely along the tranquil bends of the mighty Brahmaputra, unfolded like a breathtaking tapestry of vibrant greens, beckoning all who beheld it to pause and savour its timeless beauty. In this idyllic haven, time itself seemed to yield to the whims of nature, slowing its relentless march to a gentle, unhurried rhythm.

For our writer, Disangmukh held a significance that transcended mere geography; it was a cherished wellspring of cherished memories, a sentimental link to his ancestral past that tugged at the very core of his heart. Each visit to this ethereal village was a profound journey back in time, a cherished opportunity to reconnect with the rich tapestry of stories and legends woven by his revered elders throughout the tapestry of his youth.

On this particular day, as the writer went on a leisurely stroll through the narrow, winding lanes of Disangmukh, he found himself irresistibly drawn to the enchanting tales that seemed to whisper through the rustling leaves of ancient trees. These were not just any stories, but the captivating narratives of Baak and Dhanguli—tales of ethereal spirits, otherworldly encounters, and supernatural wonders that had long haunted his imaginative childhood dreams.

Yet, on this day, a different kind of curiosity seized hold of his inquisitive mind—a yearning to explore a tale unlike any other that had come before it. It was a story that beckoned him with an irresistible allure, a saga unburdened by spirits or mythical beings, but rather one that revolved around a living, breathing enchantress named Oikoli. Her name had lingered tantalizingly in the air, spoken in hushed tones by the villagers who guarded the secrets of Disangmukh. It was said that her beauty knew no equal, that her very presence possessed the power to ensnare even the most rational of minds.

As the writer meandered through the village, his steps guided by an unyielding curiosity, he could no longer resist the insistent call of the enigmatic Oikoli. He had heard fragments of her story, snippets of rumours, and whispers of her fabled allure, but to truly unravel the tapestry of her existence, he knew he had to venture to the source itself.

Coming to a sudden halt, he turned his gaze toward a group of villagers engaged in animated conversation beneath the comforting shade of a Silk Cotton tree. It was evident that they were deeply immersed in discussing the legends and lore that pervaded every nook and cranny of Disangmukh, and the writer recognized this as the opportune moment to embark upon his quest for knowledge. Approaching the gathering with a sense of quiet reverence, his heart fluttering with anticipation, he respectfully addressed them, his voice carrying the weight of his yearning. "Excuse me," he ventured, his words laced with a gentle urgency, "I have been captivated by the tales that speak of an exceedingly beautiful Misings**Koneng** named Oikoli. Might you kindly share with me the intricacies of her story and shed light upon the illustrious family to which she belongs?"

The villagers exchanged knowing glances, their eyes gleaming with the wisdom passed down through countless generations. It was as if the mere mention of Oikoli's name had unlocked a treasure trove of captivating stories and ancestral wisdom. Among them, the eldest, a man whose flowing beard mirrored the pristine white of the Brahmaputra's foamy crests, spoke with an air of authority that commanded attention.

"Ah, Oikoli,"he began, his voice a harmonious blend of reverence and sagacity, "hers is a tale that has ensnared the hearts of many. She hails from the illustrious **Yein** clan of MorisutiDisangmukh, and her beauty stands as a matchless testament to the legends that embrace her very being. I plead you, my friend, to take a seat amidst our humble gathering, and we shall regale you with the enchanting odyssey that is the life of Oikoli."

And so, beneath the sheltering canopy of the majestic Silk Cotton tree, surrounded by the susurrus of leaves and the echoes of ancestral tales, the writer's extraordinary journey unfolded—a voyage that would transport him beyond the boundaries of rivers and seas, deep into the heart of Disangmukh, and into the mesmerizing tapestry of love and longing that defined the enigmatic Oikoli.

CHAPTER 2

Disangmukh- The Epicentre

> *"There is a pleasure in the pathless woods, there is a rapture on the lonely shore, there is a society where none intrudes, by the deep sea, and music in its roar."* - **Lord Byron,** **'Childe Harold's Pilgrimage'**

***P**robablyin the year 1890, the river Brahmaputra, a serpentine deity of water, wound its way through the heart of Assam, cradling within its sinuous embrace the village of Disangmukh. Here, the Misings people, a tapestry of souls woven from the very essence of the river, lived in harmony with the ebb and flow of nature's caprices.*

The Taleng Okum,(kareOkum) their homes, stood proudly upon the banks, raised high on bamboo stilts as if to pay homage to the heavens. Thatched roofs, the colour of golden wheat, crowned these abodes, sheltering generations of laughter, sorrow, and dreams. The spring breeze, a playful artist, danced through the reeds and kangrass, painting the landscape with a symphony of whispers and rustles.

It was said, and not without a hint of pride, that the rhythmic beating of clothes upon the wooden planks by the village women could traverse the breadth of the Brahmaputra, carrying with it stories soaked in the suds of their daily toil. Across the river, their kin in what is now known as Majuli, would nod in silent acknowledgment of the day's labours.

Enveloped by the protective arms of towering reeds and the majestic Simolu trees, the Mising houses were a testament to the ingenuity of their people. A single-piece wooden ladder, cut from the heart of the forest, connected earth to home, a bridge between the mundane and the sanctified.

Beneath these elevated *sanctuaries, pigs and cows found respite from the sun's zealous rays, while above, families boasted large stocks of animals. The cowsheds, a stone's throw from the houses, were more than mere shelters; they were the crucibles of life, where the dung of beasts turned to gold,*

enriching the orchards with the promise of bountiful harvests.

Fruits, diverse and succulent, hung from the branches like jewels, and medicinal herbs, the legacy of ancient wisdom, grew in abundance, ready to be plucked and utilized in the myriad of festivities that marked the Misings calendar.

The Misings were rich, not in the coins of the realm, but in the wealth of the land and the livestock that roamed the vast grazing fields. Dense forests stood guard around their pastures, a green fortress that sustained their agrarian way of life.

Yet, it was not merely sustenance that the Misings derived from their lands; it was joy, pure and unadulterated. **Apong,** the elixir of their spirit, accompanied by dried fish and smoked pork, graced their tables daily. Around the hearth, the elders gathered, cups in hand, hearts full, as they surrendered to the intoxicating embrace of their homemade brew.

The **Oinitom**, a song as ancient as the hills that cradled the river, rose from their throats, a haunting melody that seemed to merge with the very soul of the Brahmaputra. The riverbank, a living entity, hummed along, a chorus of nature and man in perfect harmony.

The young Misings damsels, hearts open as the sky above, would congregate in chosen abodes, their laughter a cascade of joy. Together with their male counterparts, they danced the Gumrag, a celebration of life's rhythm, to the beat of the drum, their feet barely touching the ground as they twirled and leapt in ecstatic abandon.

Amidst this idyllic existence, the great company ships, behemoths of wood and iron, sailed by, carrying the spoils of the land—tea and sundry goods—destined for the far-off shores of Britannia. These vessels, titans of the river, would anchor along the Brahmaputra, their presence a reminder of the world beyond the reeds.

The Britishers, who had made their dominion in the greater Sivasagar, found in Disangmukh a beauty akin to their cherished seashores. The riverine landscape, a canvas of natural splendour, became their retreat, a place where time seemed to stand still.

Intrigued by the raised bamboo and wooden houses of the Misings, the Britishers, of Scandinavian descent, saw reflections of their own ancestral homes. Disangmukh's**Brahmaputra Dockyard**, a gateway of commerce and strategy, bustled with the exchange of arms, ammunition, and the finest Assam tea.

The reeds and kangrass, the mighty ships that cleaved through the waters—all drew the curious eyes of the villagers. The weekly market at Disangmukh became a melting pot of cultures, where Misings and Britisher alike exchanged glances and goods, each a novelty to the other.

Yet, the Britishers' attempts to sow the seeds of Christianity among the Misings met with the unyielding soil of tradition. The Misingss, rooted deeply in their reverence for Donyi-Polo, remained untamed, their spirits unbridled by foreign dogma. They were Misings to the core, their culture an unbroken chain linking them to the ancestors who first settled along the Brahmaputra's embrace.

The British encroachment, a shadow looming over their way of life, was met with quiet resistance. The Misings were not ready to take 'the white man's burden,' a sentiment that ran as deep as the river itself.

As dusk approached, the villagers would often wander to the dockyard, their gazes drawn to the majestic ships that seemed like creatures from another world. It was here, amidst the confluence of river and sky, that two hearts, unknown to each other, were destined to meet, their stories yet unwritten, their futures entwined in the tapestry of Disangmukh's history.

A world of a new beginning awaited, a chapter yet to be penned in the annals of time…

Every man's life ends the same way. It is only the details of how he lived and how he died that distinguish one man from another."

----Ernest Hemingway

CHAPTER 3

The First Encounter

"She walks in beauty, like the night of cloudless climes and starry skies." - **Lord Byron, 'She Walks in Beauty'**

In the gentle embrace of the night, a dim kerosene-fueled hand lamp cast a soft, flickering glow over the reed-laden banks of the Brahmaputra. The year was 1901, and within this remote

corner of Assam, the world stood still, shrouded in the quietude of the hour. It was beneath this faint, wavering light that a fateful encounter would transpire—a moment that would forever alter the course of two lives.

The Britisher, a traveller from a distant land, was not expecting to stumble upon a sight that would defy belief amidst the reeds and rugged terrain. He moved with cautious steps, guided by the dim illumination of the lamp, the weight of the unfamiliarity pressing upon him.

As his eyes adjusted to the uncertain light, he fell upon a vision that defied description—a girl, ethereal and exquisite in her beauty. Oikoli, her name known to none but the whispering winds of Disangmukh, stood bathed in the gentle glow of the lamp's light. Her presence transcended the boundaries of culture and geography, a radiant jewel amidst the reed-laden expanse.

The Britisher, his gaze locked upon her, couldn't believe the reality before him. It was as if he had stumbled upon a myth, a mirage woven by the enchanting river itself. The line ***"There is no charm equal to tenderness of heart."***(Jane Austen,) came to his mind.He stood transfixed, his heart racing, and his mind struggling to process the existence of such unparalleled beauty amidst the tribal landscape.

In the daze of his astonishment, words spilt from his lips, spoken in the only language he knew—English. "Wow! Gorgeous!" he exclaimed, unable to contain his awe and admiration. His voice was a mere whisper in the vastness of the night, a whisper that carried the weight of his astonishment.

Oikoli, surrounded by her friends in the midst of their nightly gathering, couldn't comprehend the commotion unfolding before her. She was unaware of the man's presence, let alone his words spoken in a foreign tongue. Her bewildered gaze flitted between her friends, searching for an explanation to the inexplicable.

Meanwhile, the Bengali companion who had accompanied the Britisher into this untouched world stood between worlds, a mediator of understanding. He had watched as the Britisher's eyes met Oikoli's, as a deep fascination overtook his companion. The Bengali man, while sharing the same amazement, was also gripped by a fear—a fear that the Britisher's sudden outburst might draw the attention of the Misings people, who could react with hostility to an outsider's intrusion.

With a quick gesture, the Bengali man raised his hand, pointing his thumb in the direction of Oikoli. It was a silent communication, a way of expressing the Britisher's emotions without words. The gesture spoke of admiration and desire, a longing that transcended the barrier of language.

Oikoli, in the midst of this silent exchange, found herself giggling amid her circle of friends. Their hushed whispers filled the night, their curiosity piqued by the Britisher'sbewildering behaviour. She remarked with a touch of confusion that the man who had looked upon her must be mad or perhaps had never seen girls like them before.

Amid their amusement, Oikoli remained uncertain about how to respond. The Britisher's unexpected gaze and subsequent exclamations had left her bewildered, and she grappled with the unfamiliarity of the situation.

The Britisher, on the other hand, remained entranced by the vision before him. Unable to tear his gaze away, he fell asleep that night, his thoughts consumed by the enigmatic beauty he had encountered. Two sets of whisky had passed his lips, but it was not the spirits that clouded his mind; it was the image of Oikoli, the girl who had awakened a longing he couldn't comprehend.

With the dawn of a new day, the Britisher's mind was set on a mission—a quest to unravel the enigma that was Oikoli. He, accompanied by his Bengali companion, journeyed to the river's edge and embarked on a visit to the raised bamboo platform houses of the Misingspeople.

Yet, as they ventured deeper into Disangmukh, the Britisher couldn't escape the weight of his own thoughts. What if he encountered Oikoli again? What would be her reaction to their meeting? These questions gnawed at his consciousness, threatening to drive him to madness.

His heart ached with the desire to see her once more, to engage her in conversation, and to deepen their connection. The thought of her consumed him, and he knew that he couldn't rest until he had the chance to meet her again.

"One glimpse," he thought, **"just one glimpse could satiate my thirsty heart and bring every neuron to its proper place."**

In the woven whispers of the forthcoming chapters, you, dear reader, shall find yourselves amidst the hushed luminescence of a hand lamp, where a silent saga unfolds. Here, the tapestry of Disangmukh will come alive with the intricate dance of destiny that binds Oikoli to her Britisher—a ballet of souls that speaks without words, transcending the chasms of tongues and traditions. Their entwined fates will unfurl within these pages, painting a love so pure and powerful, that it dares to leap over the precipices that divide their worlds, leaving an eternal imprint upon the very essence of Disangmukh. Prepare to be ensnared in their enchantment, for their tale is the heartbeat of this novel, a symphony of silent promises and uncharted affections that will resonate long after the last page is turned.

-Love looks not with the eyes, but with the mind, and therefore is winged Cupid painted blind."

- William Shakespeare

CHAPTER FOUR

Cultural Clash

'Love is an irresistible desire to be irresistibly desired."

-- Robert Frost

In the heart of Disangmukh, where the Brahmaputra River flowed with the gentle cadence of tradition, the inevitable collision of cultures was about to unfold like a majestic sunrise. Two worlds, each woven from the intricate threads of customs and practices, were poised to converge in a manner that would defy the expectations of the villagers.

The British man, a towering figure clad in the unfamiliar attire of jeans, stood as an enigmatic anomaly in a world where such tall, white figures had never ventured before. His presence was akin to a riddle, a puzzle that the villagers struggled to unravel, their eyes following him with a mixture of curiosity and trepidation. Whispers rustled through the air like a gentle breeze caressing the reeds, as the villagers speculated about the purpose of this outsider's visit.

In hushed tones, they commented on his peculiar attire, the way his jeans seemed to shimmer in the sunlight, and his shoes, so polished, that they seemed to reflect the very sky above. They wondered aloud about the strange instruments he carried, and the peculiar languages he spoke, so different from the melodious rhythms of their own Assamese dialect. His presence challenged the boundaries of their understanding, and they pondered whether he was a harbinger of change or merely a fleeting anomaly in the fabric of their lives.

On the other side of this cultural chasm stood Oikoli, a village damsel of incomparable grace and beauty, her copper-coloured skin glowing with an ethereal radiance in the gentle light of dawn. Her long, luscious hair cascaded down her back like a river of silk, its dark strands glistening with a subtle sheen. When she adorned herself in the meticulously woven Mising**EgeGasor**, the traditional dress of her tribe, she became a vision of elegance that left the villagers awestruck.

But it wasn't just her physical beauty that captivated hearts; it was her simplicity, her natural charm, and the gentle warmth that radiated from her very being. Oikoli was a girl who giggled with abandon as she strolled along the riverbank at dusk, the sky above painted with vibrant hues of amber and indigo.

She was the embodiment of hospitality when she offered Apong, the traditional rice beer, and pork to guests, her smile illuminating the faces of those around her. When she engaged in the rhythmic task of thrashing rice on a wooden mortar, her morning face was like the morning dew – pure, invigorating, and full of life.

It was when she ventured to the nearby marshy pond to collect fish, clad in the worn-out Misings dress, that she truly became unparalleled. Her attire seemed to depict the lush contours of her thighs, a sight that left the villagers mesmerized yet respectful, their eyes lingering on her form with a mixture of admiration and reverence. And when the rain poured from the heavens, drenching her from head to toe, her entire being blazed with a vitality that mirrored the thunderstorm itself, her laughter echoing through the air like a symphony of joy.

Oikoli was a girl educated in the ways of her culture, deeply rooted in the practices of her tribe. She possessed a beauty that was not just skin deep, but woven into the very fabric of her existence. She was a living testament to the simplicity and natural allure of the Mising way of life, a way of life that was as gentle as the morning breeze, and as vibrant as the colours of the setting sun.

Now, shift your focus to the British man -And then there was the British man – a dreamer from a distant land, a man driven by high aspirations and ambitions. He was a visitor who had journeyed across continents, drawn by the allure of Assam's landscapes and cultures, his heart beating with a restless curiosity. In his modernity, he stood in stark contrast to the simplicity of Disangmukh, his presence a gentle disruption to the rhythms of village life.

As Oikoli and the British man's paths converged, their differences became palpable, like the gentle stirring of a summer breeze. Their conversations, mediated by Bengali companions, were a blend of awkward silences and fragmented understanding, the language barrier a hurdle they struggled to overcome. Yet, it was not the only obstacle they faced.

The cultural chasm between them yawned wide, like a river ready to swallow their budding connection. Oikoli's tribe, the Mising people, observed her involvement with the British man with a mixture of curiosity, concern, and caution. They had seen outsiders before, but none had ventured into the heart of their village with such intent, their eyes watching with a mixture of fascination and trepidation.

Some villagers whispered of the risks of this mingling, fearing that the Britisher's presence could disrupt the delicate balance of their way of life. Others were more open-minded and curious about the possibilities that this cultural exchange might bring. Yet, amid these divergent opinions, all eyes remained on Oikoli and the man from England, their love story an enigma, a tapestry unlike any that had been woven before.

The future held uncertainty, but it also promised the possibility of a love that transcended cultures and boundaries – a love story that would leave an indelible mark on the history of Disangmukh and the hearts of its people. As the sun dipped below the horizon, casting a warm orange glow over the village, the fate of Oikoli and the British man hung in the balance, their love story waiting to unfold like a majestic sunrise, a new dawn that would bring with it a promise of hope, and a future yet to be written.

CHAPTER 5

Love Blossoms

"You pierce my soul. I am half agony, half hope...I have loved none but you."

- Jane Austen, Persuasion

Within Disangmukh's tender grasp, where the Brahmaputra's hushed tones carry legacies of yore, the stage was delicately set for an encounter with fate. It was a moment poised to gently entwine the destinies of two souls, crafting an intricate mosaic of affection, blossoming resolutely amidst the dance of chance.

A villager who understood Hindi engaged in a friendly conversation with a Kolkotian man, inquiring where the village girls usually congregated. This exchange of words seemed to weave a bridge, uniting two worlds on the cusp of a momentous encounter.

And so, the British man, a figure of curiosity in this tranquil village, took his first step into this unfolding story. He introduced himself asAndriceBoklin to a Misings man, a man who seemed to understand the ebb and flow of the world. **Andrice** hailed from England, on a mission associated with the ship anchored in present-day Disangmukh.

While Andrice engaged in conversation with the man, his eyes were not confined to mere words. They roamed the corners of the village like eager explorers, seeking a glimpse of something elusive. With the help of the Kolkotian man, he pieced together the purpose of his visit to the village of **Morisuti**. Yet, his eyes remained wide open, as if they would only close when they met the gaze of Oikoloi.

With a shared purpose in mind, he engaged the Misings man in conversation, seeking the name of the girl who had bewitched him. And when he heard her name spoken, a surge of emotion washed over him. Three days had passed since he had been ensnared by the beauty of a girl who, despite her height, did not quite fit the mould of a typical Misings girl.

She was **Oikoloi**—*a girl akin to a bird, her voice a melodic enchantment, and her spirit as free as the wind.* And so, the first piece of this intricate puzzle fell into place, guided by the deft hand of fate.

Andrice, with newfound purpose, followed the Misings man and the Kolkotian deeper into the heart of the village. A message had been sent ahead to Oikoloi, a message carried on the wings of anticipation. It informed her that a guest was on his way, a guest who would accompany them to the village's **MurongOkum**—a thatched club for the village's youths.

Oikoloi, flanked by her friends, awaited this unexpected arrival. ***They gathered like a flock of birds, their laughter a harmonious melody that danced in the air.*** As the two tall men approached, Oikoloi remained hidden among her friends. Shyness enveloped her, rendering her unable to meet Andrice's gaze, ***not because she was in love with him, but because he was the man who had captured her attention on a moonlit night, far from the heart of the village.***

Andrice, though, possessed a keen eye that had not forgotten the silhouette of long hair and the enchanting copper-toned complexion. He knew, even without seeing her face, that Oikoloi was the girl he had been enchanted by for three days and three nights.

They sat on the MurongOkum, Andrice and the Kolkotian man, amidst an audience of curious onlookers. Oikoloi's bashfulness prevented her from stealing even a furtive glance at Andrice, for she recalled the night when their eyes had met across the expanse of the village, illuminated by the faint glow of a kerosene-filled hand lamp(lantern).

Andrice, too, was content to sit there, an inscrutable smile playing upon his lips as he conversed with the villagers. His eyes, however, betrayed the joy of finally being in her presence, and they lingered on her form as if tracing the contours of his beloved's face.

Here in the bosom of Disangmukh, under the watchful gaze of the Brahmaputra, a connection was thus forged—*a connection that transcended language, culture, and distance. Love had taken root, and the odds, though formidable, would not deter its growth. This was the beginning of a love story that would defy the boundaries of their worlds, a love story painted with the vibrant hues of two souls intertwining against all odds.*

"Whatever our souls are made of, his and mine are the same."

-Emily Bronte, '*Wuthering Heights*'

CHAPTER 6

Villagers' Concern

"Love recognizes no barriers. It jumps hurdles, leaps fences, penetrates walls to arrive at its destination full of hope." - Maya Angelou

In the verdant heart of Disangmukh, where the Brahmaputra's whispers cradle the village in an eternal lullaby, a love story unfolds, tender and defiant. AndriceBoklin, an

Englishman with a heart ablaze for Oikoloi, finds himself ensnared by a passion that knows no bounds of land or sea.

As Andrice wanders the village paths, his inner voice speaks to him, a monologue of longing and determination:

"Oikoloi, the very name sets my heart to a rhythm unknown before. Each syllable, has a beat that resonates with my own. How peculiar it is, that in this remote corner of the world, I should find the missing piece of my soul. The language between us is a vast river, yet in her eyes, I see the bridge we can build. Oh, how I yearn to express the depth of my affection, to weave our disparate threads into a single tapestry of love."

The MurongOkum had been the genesis of their bond, and since that auspicious encounter, Andrice's affections have refused to be content with mere fleeting observations of Oikoloi's grace. Her name, once an exotic melody, now slips from his tongue with a familiarity that warms his very soul. Amidst his sojourn in Disangmukh, he is beset by a longing to cultivate their acquaintance further, to convey the depth of his burgeoning sentiments.

"Disangmukh, you've become more than a mere waypoint on my journey; you are the crucible of my heart's most fervent desires. Each day I am here, I am drawn to her, as the moon to the tides. Oikoloi, my dear, what spell have you cast upon me?"

Oikoloi, a maiden of reflective disposition, wrestles with the tides of her own heart. Her inner thoughts are a quiet storm of contemplation and fear:

"This man, Andrice, he comes from a world so unlike my own. His eyes hold stories of distant lands, his words a melody of another life. Can I dare to dream of a life beyond the banks of the Brahmaputra? Or is my heart too deeply rooted in the soil of Disangmukh?"

The village, a lush tapestry of Kangrass and bamboo, offers no haven for lovers to meet and share the silent language of their hearts. The daylight's enchantments are reserved for the village's youth, but not for Oikoloi and Andrice. Only beneath the shroud of night can their hearts truly converge, the bamboo groves their clandestine haven.

"In the secrecy of the groves, our hands entwine, our breaths mingle. The world outside fades into shadow, and there is only Oikoloi. Her laughter, a melody that rivals the song of the river. Our stolen moments are a rebellion against the march of time, a declaration of our love's existence."

Oikoloi's friends, acting as her guardians, stood watchful at a distance, ensuring their privacy. Cloaked in secrecy, she would steal away to meet Andrice, their hearts beating in synchrony, as if guided by an ancient rhythm.

Andrice, accompanied now only by the Bengali mediator, found that their hearts had forged a language of their own—one that transcended the limitations of mere words. In the hushed whispers of the wind through the bamboo leaves, in the gentle rustle of their entwined hands, and in the stolen glances that spoke volumes, they discovered a profound connection that defied the boundaries of their respective worlds.

The bamboo groves, with their tall and slender stalks, seemed to mirror the delicate dance of their burgeoning love. Amidst the dappling moonlight that filtered through the lush foliage, Andrice and Oikoloi would lose themselves in each other's presence. It was as if the very essence of their beings resonated in harmony, entwining their souls in an ethereal embrace.

Their clandestine meetings amidst the bamboo groves became a tapestry woven with secrecy and longing. Each stolen moment deepened their bond, fueling the fire of their desire to defy the odds that sought to keep them apart. The world outside the groves faded away, and they existed in a timeless realm, where only their hearts could speak the language of love.

And so, the bamboo groves became witness to their hidden whispers and stolen kisses, holding their secrets close, like the nocturnal spirits that danced among the shadows. It was within this sanctuary that Andrice and Oikoloi discovered the power of their love—a love that thrived in the midst of adversity, nurtured by the very barriers that sought to confine it.

Their eyes became the messengers of their affection, eloquent in their silent exchange. In those stolen moments, they discovered a world where words were unnecessary, where the language of the heart was more profound than any uttered sounds.

With the assistance of the Bengali gentleman, Andrice's declaration reaches Oikoloi. His departure looms, a mere week away, but his heart's declaration cannot wait—he cherishes Oikoloi, and he desires her hand in matrimony.

"Oikoloi, my heart's companion, the days may be few, but my love is boundless. I stand before you, a man of another world, asking you to join me in mine. Together, we can forge a new path, one that winds like the Brahmaputra itself—unpredictable, but beautiful."

As their hearts begin to weave an intricate web of emotion, a bridge is gradually erected, spanning the vast gulf between their unfamiliar cultures. They find themselves lost in one another, transcending the boundaries of their worlds. Meanwhile, whispers circulate amongst the villagers, their thoughts ensnared by the burgeoning romance.

As the evening descended upon Disangmukh, the villagers gathered under the thatched roofs of their houses, their faces illuminated by the flickering light of the lanterns. The air was thick with concern and the murmur of voices as the community delved into the matter of Miss Oikoli and Mr. Boklin's burgeoning romance.The young men of the village gathered around the flickering flames, their faces illuminated by the dance of firelight. The topic of the young woman's romance with the foreign Englishman was the kindling that fueled their spirited debate.

"She has caught the eye of many," whispered one, his gaze lost in the fire. *"I've seen the way she moves through the village—like a gentle breeze. Many hearts here ache for her."*

Another interjected, his voice tinged with practicality, *"But what of this outsider? He is not of our world. She belongs here, with us, not in some distant land that we know nothing of."*

"Yet, who are we to cage her heart?" countered another, always the dreamer among them. *"Love is a wild bird; it cannot be tamed. If her heart soars with him, should we not wish them to fly together?"*

The conversation took a darker turn as one suggested, *"This Englishman disrupts the balance of our lives. Perhaps he should find himself lost in the forest, away from her, away from Disangmukh."*

An uneasy silence fell upon the group, the crackling of the fire punctuating their thoughts. It was the wise elder, who had been listening from a distance, who spoke with the authority of his years:

"Remember, that the forest is not ours to wield as a weapon. Our traditions teach us the sanctity of life and the freedom to follow one's heart. We must not let fear drive us to darkness."

The youths nodded, the wisdom of the elder's words quelling the storm within their hearts. They knew that whatever their personal desires, the young woman's happiness was a choice that belonged to her alone, a sacred right that no one could deny.

In various households throughout the village, the air was filled with the sound of discussions among the elderly men, who sat together sharing bowls of Apong and plates of 'RomnamSanne' Ongo (heated dry fish).

"I tell you, it's not right," grumbled an elder, his voice carrying the weight of years. *"Our Oikoli, with an outsider? What will become of our traditions?"*

A young man, his eyes alight with the fire of youth, spoke up, *"But elder, love does not know such boundaries. Should we not wish for Oikoli's happiness above all?"*

The elder shook his head, *"Happiness, yes, but at what cost? Must we forsake our ways for this... this infatuation?"*

From the edge of the circle, a woman's voice rose, strong and clear, *"We must think of Oikoli's future. This Englishman, he will leave, and then what? She will be left with nothing but a broken heart and whispers behind her back."*

Another villager, a middle-aged man with a thoughtful expression, chimed in, *"We cannot decide for her. It is her heart, her choice. Have we not raised our children to be free, like the river?"*

The conversation ebbed and flowed like the Brahmaputra itself, with opinions as varied as the leaves on the trees. Some spoke of opportunity and change, others of honour and the preservation of their culture.

"What of Oikoli's parents? What do they say?" asked a young woman, her voice tinged with concern.

"They are torn," replied another villager. *"They fear for her, yet they see the love in her eyes. It is a difficult choice."*

As the night deepened, the voices melded into a chorus of concern, each villager invested in the outcome of this unlikely love story. Andrice, halfsleeping just beyond the Marisuti felt like listening to the voices of Disangmukh, their words a testament to the challenge he and Oikoli faced.

"Oikoli, my dear," he whispered to the night, *"whatever the morrow brings, my heart is yours. We shall face the dawn together, come what may."*

The fate of Oikoli and Andrice hung in the balance, their love story a mirror reflecting the village's struggle between the comfort of tradition and the winds of change. In Disangmukh, where the river's whispers spoke of ages past, their love awaited its destiny, ready to bloom or wither in the soil of time.

'In love, there are two things—bodies and words."

-Joyce Carol Oates

Mising Oini:tom

Kangkanéna Kangkanéna
Sí:sang Oibí kangkané

Apin doma:p du:la:dag
Oimé ka:ma:p du:la:mang

Translated English Meaning:

(Fair and lovely, oh youthful beloved, your beauty shines true,/Meals I may skip, but a day without your sight, I simply cannot do.)

CHAPTER SEVEN

I have for the first time found what I can truly love—I have found you. You are my sympathy—my better self— my good angel.”
Charlotte Bronte, *Jane Eyre*.

The Proposal

As he sat deep in contemplation, Andrice's mind swirling with thoughts and questions, a sudden interruption shattered the tranquillity of the moment. A voice, unexpected and jarring, pierced through the silence, cutting through the layers of his introspection. Startled, he looked up, searching for the source of this unwelcome intrusion. In the bustling dockyard, amidst the clatter of machinery and the shouts of labourers, there stood a Bengali man. He was a fellow worker, toiling away with Andrice, their paths often crossing as they went about their daily tasks. With keen eyes, he had noticed the unmistakable signs of turmoil etched upon Andrice's face. With a flicker of curiosity in his eyes, the Bengali man leaned forward and posed a question that hung in the air, laden with concern. *"What is your next move?"* he inquired, his voice laced with a hint of urgency.

In the quiet solitude of his study, Andrice found solace in the presence of a trusted confidant. Grateful for the opportunity to unburden himself, he didn't waste a moment before opening up his heart. With a heavy heart, he revealed his predicament, his words laced with a touch of desperation. *"I am bound to wed Oikoli, or at the very least, resolve this matter before my departure to Kolkata and England,"* he confessed. The room was dimly lit, the air heavy with anticipation. Andrice, a young man with a determined look in his eyes, turned to his trusted friend, Bengali Babu, seeking his assistance in this daring endeavour. **"Bengali Babu,"**Andrice implored, his voice filled with urgency, *"you must lend me your aid in this noble pursuit."* Andrice, a man of heart ached at the mere notion of leaving her behind. The weight of the decision pressed heavily upon him, threatening to consume his every thought. How could he bear to part ways with the one who had captured his soul? As he gazed into her eyes, he saw a reflection of his own torment. The love they shared was undeniable, a bond that had weathered countless storms. Yet, circumstances had conspired.

In the cloak of darkness, two figures stood close, their bodies pressed together as they whispered in low tones. The silence of the night enveloped them, lending an air of secrecy to their conversation. With determination burning in their hearts, they huddled together, their minds brimming with ideas. A plan, they knew, was the key to success. And so, they devised a cunning strategy, one that would take them on a journey to the nearby Misings village of Disangmukh. Their goal was clear - to win over the elders and villagers, to forge a bond that would transcend differences and unite them in a common purpose. The road ahead was treacherous, filled with uncertainty and challenges, but they were undeterred. Each step they took brought them closer to their destination, their hearts pounding with a mix of excitement. Their strategy was a cunning one, devised to ensure their seamless integration into the fabric of the local community. With a calculated finesse, they sought to mingle effortlessly with the locals, effortlessly blending in like a chameleon in its natural habitat. To achieve this, they brought forth *a precious offering - imported whisky, a bar of liquid gold that held the promise of camaraderie and shared moments.* ***With each bottle carefully selected, they aimed to forge connections, break down barriers, and win***

the trust of those they encountered. Yet, their approach was not one of overt persuasion or forceful imposition. No, they understood the delicate dance required to gain acceptance. It was a subtle art, a dance of subtlety and grace. They knew that true integration could not be forced, however, a significant challenge loomed over the villagers as they found themselves faced with an unfamiliar presence - foreign spirits. Their customary drink, **Apong,** had always been their trusted companion, but now they were forced to confront the unknown. The air was thick with uncertainty, as the villagers grappled with this new and unexpected development. How would they adapt to these foreign spirits, so different from what they had known for generations? It was a question that weighed heavily on their minds, casting a shadow of doubt over their once peaceful village.

Andrice and the Bengali man, both foreigners in this riverine village, found themselves captivated by the allure of its vibrant culture. With genuine- enthusiasm, they eagerly embraced the chance to fully engage in the daily lives of the villagers. *Their goal was simple-: gain a profound understanding of the villagers' customs and traditions.* However, as they delved deeper into the core of this close-knit community, an undeniable feeling of scepticism seemed to hang in the air. **It was as if generations of mistrust and wariness had become not just a part of their collective consciousness, but also ingrained within their very beings.**

Andrice and his companion were intrigued by this discovery, for it hinted at a complex history that had shaped the villagers' outlook on life. They wondered what experiences had led them to adopt such a sceptical mindset, and how it had influenced their interactions with the outside world. As they stepped into the tight-knit community where Oikoli grew up, a significant majority, **eighty per cent to be exact**, held firm in their opposition to her plans of marrying a **'kamponTani,'** *a white man, and venturing off to a faraway land like England.* The idea of such a union and departure seemed to stir up a storm of disapproval among the village folks, who clung tightly to their traditional values and way of life. ***The winds of change blew through the riverine kangrass, whispering tales of transformation and upheaval.*** The people, accustomed to the familiar rhythm of their lives, felt a shiver of fear crawl up their spines. Change, especially of such magnitude, was a formidable force that stirred unease in their hearts. *Resistance, like a stubborn weed*, sprouted in the minds of the townsfolk. They clung to the comfort of the known, fearing the unknown that lay beyond the horizon of their existence.

Amidst the vast expanse of uncertainty, a glimmer of optimism shone through. In the quaint village, a subtle shift in attitudes was observed, as if the winds of change were gently blowing through the narrow streets. **It was whispered among the villagers that a union was on the horizon, one that would bridge the gap between cultures and bring an outsider into their close-knit community.**

Curiosity and intrigue danced in the eyes of approximately forty per cent of the villagers, their hearts open to the possibility of a son-in-law from a distant land. The idea of having a foreigner as a member of their own family seemed to ignite a spark of excitement within them. They envisioned a future where their grandchildren, with their fair skin and English tongues, would bring a touch of the unknown to their humble abode. Whispers of this union spread like wildfire, weaving their way through the village, reaching every corner and every ear. The villagers, with their minds buzzing with anticipation, wondered how this union would unfold and what it would mean for their tight-knit community.

Andrice, a young and ambitious individual, found himself faced with a challenging situation. He understood that a strategic approach was necessary to achieve his goals. With this in mind, he made a calculated decision to direct his efforts towards Oikoli's father, a man who held considerable influence within their community. With the sun casting long shadows across the bustling streets of Kolkata, he found himself in the company of a kind-hearted Bengali man. Together, they embarked on a mission that held great significance - to win over the heart of Oikoli's father, a man whose influence held the power to shape their destiny. As they walked through the narrow lanes, the air was filled with the aroma of spices and the vibrant chatter of the locals. The Bengali man, with his deep understanding of the local customs and traditions, became his guiding light in this unfamiliar territory. Their destination was a grand mansion, not of bricks but of Bamboo, wooden pieces and thatched roofs nestled amidst a lush forest, where Oikoli's father resided. The man's reputation preceded him - a formidable figure, known for his discerning nature and unwavering determination. Winning his approval was no easy feat, but they were determined to give it their all. With each step closer toOikoli's love.

Andrice, with a gentle smile on his face, approached Oikoli's father, his hand tightly clutching a small bundle. As he stood before him, a mixture of nervousness and excitement danced in his eyes. With a deep breath, he extended his arm, offering a modest sum of money as a token of his affection. The room fell silent, the air thick with anticipation. Oikoli's father, a stern man with a weathered face, looked at Andrice with a mixture of surprise and gratitude. His eyes softened as he accepted the gift, his fingers delicately tracing the edges of the money. Oikoli's eyes widened with astonishment as she gazed upon the precious offering. It was a symbol of their love, a token that spoke volumes of Boklin's dedication to her and her family. The villagers whispered in awe, their voices hushed in reverence for the extraordinary gesture unfolding before them. In that moment, the air seemed to hold its breath, In the quaint village, where time seemed to move at a leisurely pace, a most intriguing gesture captivated the hearts and minds of its inhabitants. It was an offering that held a certain allure, one that had never before graced the humble abodes and reeds-filled **Marisuti**. The object of fascination? A bottle of exquisite whisky, a luxury that had remained elusive to the villagers until that very moment. Its presence alone spoke volumes, whispering promises of indulgence and sophistication.

Under the shroud of night, Andrice and the mysterious Bengali man found themselves engaged in a series of profound conversations with Oikoli's family. The air was thick with anticipation as they delved into the depths of their hearts, sharing their hopes, fears, and dreams. Each word uttered carried a weight as if the very essence of their souls hung in the balance. The moon cast a gentle glow upon their faces, illuminating the intensity in their eyes as they forged a connection that transcended language and cultural barriers. In that moment, time seemed to stand still, as the world outside faded away, leaving only the profound bond that was forming between these unlikely companions. As the amber liquid poured freely from the bottles, its smooth, golden streams mingled with the air, casting a warm, inviting glow upon the gathering. The room buzzed with an infectious energy, as laughter and animated conversations filled every corner. With each passing moment, the atmosphere grew more convivial, as friends and acquaintances alike found solace in the company of one another. The clinking of brass bowls and the gentle

During the lively conversation, Andrice, with a determined gleam in their eyes, took a resolute step forward. With a determined gaze, he looked into the eyes of Oikoli's family, assuring them of his unwavering commitment. The room was filled with anticipation as he spoke, his words carrying the weight of a solemn promise. He expressed his willingness to embark on a journey that would bind their lives together, a journey guided by the customs and rituals that held deep significance for their family. His voice resonated with sincerity as he pledged to honour and respect their cherished traditions. Each word he uttered was carefully chosen, carrying the weight of his devotion. It was clear that he understood the importance of upholding their heritage, and he embraced it wholeheartedly. The family members exchanged glances, their faces reflecting a mixture of relief and gratitude. They had longed for a partner who would not only accept their customs but also embrace them as his own. In this young man, they saw a beacon of hope, someone who would safeguard their traditions and ensure their continuation for generations. With a glimmer in his eyes, he spoke passionately, emphasising the profound impact their union could have. It wasn't just about their own happiness, but the potential for acceptance from the sceptical villagers. He believed that their love had the power to bridge the divide, to dissolve the barriers that had long separated their families. It was a dream he held close to his heart, a dream that whispered of a future where love triumphed over prejudice. In the dimly lit room, two figures sat across from each other, their eyes locked in a silent battle of emotions. It was a negotiation unlike any other, one that delicately balanced the tender tendrils of love with the heavy burden of societal expectations. She, a woman of grace and elegance, wore a mask of composure that hid the turmoil within her heart. Her every movement exuded a quiet strength, a determination to defy the norms that threatened to confine her. Yet, her eyes betrayed a flicker of vulnerability, a longing for a love that transcended the

As the moon rose high in the sky, casting a soft glow over the village, Andrice and the Bengali man found themselves at the end of a long and eventful evening. The air was filled with a sense of anticipation as if the night had whispered secrets that only they could hear. With their minds still buzzing from the discussions that had taken place, Andrice and the Bengali man exchanged knowing glances. It was as if a flame had been ignited within them, a flame fueled by the collective hope that had filled the room. They could feel it coursing through their veins, warming their hearts and lifting their spirits. Leaving the village behind, they embarked on a journey that held the promise of change. Each step they took was filled with determination, their souls Andrice gazed out into the darkness of the night, feeling as though time had slowed down. Each passing moment seemed to stretch on, prolonging the wait that lay ahead. But this was no ordinary restlessness; it was a fervent anticipation, a yearning that pulsed through Andrice's veins. In the depths of their heart, Andrice longed to hold Oikoli in their arms, to feel the warmth of their embrace and to solidify their love in a way that would be recognised and accepted by all. It was a desire that went beyond mere affection; it was a craving for the union of their souls, bound by the sacred bonds of tradition and societal approval.

CHAPTER **8**

Wedding Preparations

"We are each other's harvest; we are each other's business; we are each other's magnitude and bond."

- Gwendolyn Brooks

(Pulitzer Prize-winning author of *Annie Allen*)

The village of Disangmukh hummed with anticipation as the news of Oikoli's impending nuptials spread like wildfire. In the heart of the village, beneath the sprawling bushes of the Bamboo trees, **Lilen** and **Riyad** found solace in their familiar meeting spot. Their faces, etched with worry and longing, gazed out at the village they cherished. "Can you fathom it, Riyad?" Lilen's voice trembled, a mixture of disbelief and sorrow colouring his words. "Our dear Oikoli is to be wed to a British man from beyond our humble village. It feels as though a part of our world will vanish with her departure." Riyad nodded, his eyes anchored to the ground, his voice laden with emotion. ***"Indeed, Lilen, Oikoli has always been the essence of our lives. It's difficult to envision Disangmukh without her radiant spirit."*** Meanwhile, within the walls of **Oikoli**'s home, preparations for the wedding were underway with fervent zeal. The air buzzed with energy as palpable as the unspoken melancholy in the hearts of the relatives who gathered to fulfil their duties with unwavering devotion. They knew their role was to ensure a proper traditional wedding—an occasion that demanded their utmost respect and diligence. Oikoli's middle-aged parents found solace in a single ray of hope amidst their tangled emotions. Anrice, the British suitor, had graciously declined any dowry, affirming that his desire lay solely in Oikoli's hand in marriage. This heartfelt gesture had been conveyed through the assistance of a well-regarded BangaliBabu, who bridged the cultural divide with his eloquence. The immediate task for Oikoli's family was to gather the necessary ingredients for the grand feast—a culinary extravaganza that would stand as a testament to their heritage.

The mind's eye captures the vibrant scenes within the bustling kitchen: the fragrant waft of spices and herbs mingling with the rhythmic clatter of cooking utensils, as skilled hands-crafted dishes steeped in tradition. The scene pulsed with the essence of tribal cuisine, its flavours derived from the bountiful offerings of the land.

Now, let's have a vision of the family's orchard, a verdant sanctuary brimming with life. Lush betel nut trees swayed gently in the breeze, their emerald leaves shimmering in the sunlight. Here, readers can focus on the abundant betel leaves, ready to be plucked and woven into the fabric of the wedding customs. Beyond the orchard, the surrounding forests beckoned with promises of leafy reeds and medicinal herbs, their presence adding depth and complexity to the forthcoming feast. The word of the wedding preparations spread rapidly through the village, igniting a collective sense of responsibility and unity. One by one, the villagers emerged from their homes, their hearts alight with love for Oikoli and reverence for tradition. Each household pledged their support, promising to contribute two pitchers of Apong—a testament to their understanding of Oikoli's family's time constraints. The villagers' resolute assurances eased the burden on the family, confident that the Boars and an abundance of dry fish would be procured without difficulty.

As the sun began its descent, casting a warm golden glow upon the village, there was a scene of unwavering dedication. Oikoli's family and the villagers wrought tirelessly, their hands moving in harmonious rhythm, weaving a tapestry of love and tradition. We came to a close with a sweeping panorama of the village, now bathed in the soft hues of twilight. It served as a poignant reminder of the transformative power of unity and the profound impact that a wedding steeped in tradition could have on the collective soul of a community.

"Tradition is not the worship of ashes, but the preservation of fire."

– Gustav Mahler

CHAPTER 9

The Wedding

"Love is the emblem of eternity; it confounds all notion of time; effaces all memory of a beginning, all fear of an end."– **Madame de Stael**

In the dimming light of the evening, amidst the groves of bamboo that had stood sentinel over the village of Marisuti,

Disangmukh for generations, two old men sat hunched over their bowls of Apong. Their hands, etched with the lines of many harvests, cradled the bowls with a tenderness that spoke of their deep respect for the traditional brew. Yet, their minds were not on the familiar comfort of the rice beer today; their conversation, subdued and serious, was focused on the morrow's unprecedented event.

"Tomorrow, our Oikoli will become an outsider's wife,"* murmured the first, *his voice a blend of sorrow and disapproval. "No boy from our village could capture her heart. **Ngokké Asinsé aipé mídérdag, ngo:lukké dolungso:k ai:né konengko amilo: Gípakyé** *(I am disheartened to see that one good girl from the village will no longer be with us as she will marry an outsider"*

The second old man nodded, his eyes reflecting the flicker of the nearby oil lamp. "It sets a bad precedent, allowing an outsider to infiltrate our customs and traditions. What if more of our daughters follow her lead?"

They both knew the answer, yet they feared it. **The unity of the Mising people was at stake, and this wedding could be the pebble that disturbed the still waters of their community.**

Meanwhile, the air around Oikoli's house was thick with the scent of festivities. Misings people, their faces bright with excitement and hands busy with preparations were coming and going. Men were seen cutting pork, their knives glinting in the sun, while others collected leafy vegetables, soft reeds, and medicinal herbs to be mixed with the pork dishes. The dry fishes were put over the fire flame, their skins crackling as they turned golden and edible.

The village women, their laughter mingling with the clink of pots, were busy distilling rice beer. The cone-like pots bubbled with promise, and many old men, their taste for the white variety of rice beer (Apong) undiminished by time, eagerly awaited their morning bowl mixed with hot tea—a tradition savoured before heading to the paddy fields.

And there, in the midst of it all, was Oikoli. *Dressed in the traditional Mising attire of Kampon(white)Ege and Gasor, she radiated a beauty that needed no enhancement from lipstick or rouge. Her friends, who had shared in her secret meetings with Andrice, now giggled and whispered, reminiscing about the fearsome yet unforgettable moments they had witnessed. Oikoli, however, asked them to hold their tongues; this was not the time for such tales.*

The door of her house was adorned with garlands of **mango leaves, interspersed with**

pink and white flowers plucked fresh from the garden. It was a threshold that marked the end of one life and the beginning of another.

Across the village, Andrice stood alone but for the company of the Bengali Babu. Through Oikoli, the Bengali man had procured a Misings dress for the groom—GonroUgon and MibuGaluk. The white traditional loincloth, GonroUgon, was a bit short for Andrice's towering figure, but it was worn with pride. Led by the Bengali Babu, Andrice made his way to the wedding house, his heart a mix of anticipation and a foreigner's anxiety.

As he ascended the raised bamboo platform of the wedding house, he was greeted by the sight of various food items: pork, dry fish, and boiled herbs with pig's blood. The sticky rice flavoured with local chicken sent an alluring vapour into the air, signalling the feast to come.

The village priests, akin to Shammans, offered blessings in the presence of the village elders, who were engrossed in drinking Apong and partaking in the feast's first offerings. The names of Donyi-Po:lo: were shouted in unison, blessing the couple in the age-old tradition of the Misings people.

After the rituals, the villagers sat together, the feast uniting them in celebration. The young boys and girls, with their drums and Gumrag dance, transformed the atmosphere. The British groom was coaxed into the dance, his hands raised in an attempt to follow the rhythm of Oin:itom and Gumrag. For a moment, the village forgot what they were about to lose.

But the time for farewells had come. The air was heavy with the sound of crying, weeping, and sobbing. Andrice, though he understood the scene's gravity, could not convey his promise to keep Oikoli happy and content. He asked the Bengali man to speak on his behalf, to assure the villagers of his duty-bound commitment to their beloved Oikoli.

As the bullock cart began to move, taking Oikoli away from her Marisuti home, discussions arose among the menfolk about where the couple would stay before their eventual journey to England. Concern was etched on every face, yet the cart moved on, and Oikoli's sobs were carried away in the wind.

But for **Oikoli**, the rhythm of Bullock cart's movement seemed to echo the pulse of her heart. In this moment of transition, the song that has been woven into the fabric of her life rose unbidden in her memory:

**"Ba:bu oi usatagTorjípo:rangongoki,
Na:níbí oi usatakpinbagoyyoiapinoki!
Biro-bírmangbísatakLí:négenépe:reyoki
Kumrí-
doríbísatakmé:nyokmanamayangoki."**

The song, a mosaic of her upbringing, fills her with a flood of recollections. Each line is a thread connecting her to the family she's leaving behind. ***The uncle who nurtured her*** *with skillfully harvested fish, the aunts who nourished her with portions of leftover cooked rice, the siblings who carried her swathed in vibrant garments, and the neighbours whose affection left an indelible imprint on her soul.*

As the cart moves farther away, the song becomes a vivid tapestry in her mind, each verse a colour, each memory a stroke of the brush painting her past. The song is not just a melody; it is the embodiment of her heritage, a lyrical narrative of her life's journey thus far.

In the midst of her inner turmoil, the song offers a semblance of solace, a reminder that although she is leaving, the essence of her home remains within her. It's a bittersweet farewell, a silent serenade that will continue to resonate within Oikoli, accompanying her as she ventures into the new chapter of her life.

"Love knows not its own depth until the hour of separation."

– Kahlil Gibran

CHAPTER 10

Only Two

In vain I have struggled. It will not do. My
feelings will not be repressed. You must allow
me to tell you how ardently I admire and love
you."

— **Jane Austen**, *Pride and Prejudice*

Beneath the moon's vigilant gaze,
Andrice and Oikoli spun a sanctuary of whispers
and dreams within the ship's chamber—a realm
where the clamour of the world dwindled to a
tender murmur. Moonlight pirouetted through the
window, an accomplice in silence to their love,

draping them in a cloak of silver, their shadows painting a tender mural upon the timbers.

In this hushed harbour, two hearts from worlds apart discovered a shared rhythm. Andrice, rooted in British soil, and Oikoli, the bloom of Disangmukh, stood on the brink of a shared tomorrow. The bamboo groves and riverbanks, once guardians of their secret exchanges, now lay behind them as relics of a time before. Oikoli was entirely his, their love an unyielding bastion against the relentless currents of destiny.

Andrice's arms were a haven, a stronghold for Oikoli as if he cradled a delicate bird that might, at any moment, take flight. Her initial reserve, a whisper of her past, soon dissolved into the certainty of his embrace. They nestled together in a small room aboard the docked ship, a sanctuary where their love unfurled its wings, far from the shadows and whispers of the world outside.

In the quietude, *Andrice pondered, his heart swelling with a silent vow. "In this silentchamber, where the world outside becomes a distant murmur,*

I find my truth in your eyes. Oikoli, my heart's compass, guiding me through uncharted waters. Here, in the cradle of our whispers, I vow to be your anchor, your haven, as we sail into the dawn of our shared destiny."

Words were too meagre for Andrice's storm of feelings; he chose the eloquence of silence instead. He cradled Oikoli, each heartbeat a precious note in their symphony. When her eyes, pools of inquiry, sought his voice, he answered with a smile and a hug that spoke in the tongue of eternity. The night was their canvas, and their love,and the artist, eager to paint its masterpiece.

As the moon's gentle caress stirred memories within Oikoli, she found herself caught in a monologue of reminiscence and longing. ***"The river calls to me, a siren song of the life I once knew. Can you fathom the silent storm within me? As I stand here, draped in the fabric of my heritage, I am torn between the echoes of Disangmukh and the allure of distant shores. Yet, in your embrace, I find the courage to weave our future from the threads of hope and the colours of dawn."***

The moon's gentle caress stirred memories within Oikoli—echoes of laughter with friends, the rhythm of life in the Murongokum. Her village, a heartbeat away, now belonged to a chapter closed. Through the ship's narrow gaze, they beheld the moon's twilight, a celestial embrace that wrapped around them. Their souls, entwined, surrendered to the night's lullaby and slipped into dreams.

With the dawn's whisper, Oikoli awoke, her spirit cloaked in thought. A silent weight pressed upon her, a secret nestled deep within. Andrice, feeling her absence like a missing note in a melody, sought her presence. He found her outside, her gaze lost on the horizon. The call of the river was strong, and she longed for the privacy of its embrace. With a tender plea, she beckoned Andrice to be her shield against prying eyes, to find solace on the river's far shore.

Cleansed by the river's touch, Oikoli adorned herself in the Egegasor, her beauty a testament to tradition. The Bengali man, their voice across the language divide, wove their words together. They strolled by the river, Oikoli's past unfurling before Andrice, her finger tracing the memories of fish caught and days bathed in the glow of water hyacinths.

Watching Oikoli by the river, Andrice reflected silently, "There she stands, the river's daughter, her beauty untamed as the waters that cradle her reflection. Your past is a tapestry rich with the hues of home. Together, we'll write our story, a narrative that flows like the river—endless and ever true."

Time flowed like the river, and soon they stood before her kin in Disangmukh. With the Bengali man's help, they spoke of voyages and new horizons. Oikoli's heart wrestled with unspoken words, her thoughts a silent song: ***"Ngo kapeAndricekeleduloagomsemluposuen, kapeasinagomkirisem be kinyen."*** How to translate the language of her heart? Yet, she held fast to hope, believing that love's melody would grow fuller with time, binding them in an unbreakable harmony.

CHAPTER 11

A Bittersweet Departure: Way to England

We could never have loved the earth so well if we had had no childhood in it...

-George Eliot, (The Mill on the Floss)

The day had come. Oikoli stood at the edge of Disangmukh, her heart heavy with emotion. The reality of leaving everything behind weighed upon her, threatening to engulf her in a sea of nostalgia. Tears welled up in her eyes as she thought about Marisuti, her dear friend whom she would never see again. Her dreams and aspirations, nurtured in this village, would remain here, forever etched in her memory.

"Marisuti, my sister in spirit," she whispered to the wind, "our shared laughter and tears will remain rooted in this soil. How can I step onto this ship without a piece of my soul tearing away? Yet, I carry our memories, like precious gems, close to my heart."

As the ship prepared to set sail for England, Oikoli's gaze lingered on the river that had been her companion throughout her life. The lush green kangrass swaying in the breeze, the towering silk cotton tree, and the camaraderie of her friends during fish catching—all would become distant memories. Even the wooden mortar, her early morning companion while pounding rice and the gentle grunting sounds of the piglets beneath the raised bamboo platform would be left behind.

"Brahmaputra, you have witnessed my life unfold from the innocence of childhood to the precipice of this moment," she mused, her eyes tracing the flow of the river. "Your waters carry my reflection, a mirror to my soul. As I leave, know that each ripple tells a story of the life I've lived."

Yet, amidst the poignant farewells, Oikoli found the strength to embrace the unknown. She knew that destiny had written a new chapter for her, and she was ready to step into it with unwavering courage. She held onto the belief that wherever life took her, her spirit would remain connected to her roots, carrying the essence of Disangmukh within her.

Oikoli's cries echoed across the river, a pure expression of her rustic sorrow that resonated with the birds and the entire landscape. The birds, the swallows, and every creature seemed to join in her mournful symphony as if they too would miss her dearly. Amidst this chorus, a lone bird soared high above, its melodious song carrying a message of hope and resilience.

"Farewell, my feathered friends, keepers of my village's songs," she said softly, watching the bird's ascent. "Your flight inspires me to rise above my sorrow. May your wings carry my prayers for those I leave behind."

As the ship embarked on its westward journey, Oikoli's tears began to subside. Andrice, understanding her emotional turmoil, enveloped her in a gentle embrace, providing solace and reassurance. His body language spoke volumes, conveying his unwavering care and love.

As the ship sailed, they marvelled at the riverine beauty of the mighty Brahmaputra. Oikoli, for a brief moment, remained silent, tilting her head towards her village, catching a fleeting glimpse of the place she called home. Andrice, by her side, offered a supportive presence, understanding the significance of this moment. His eyes met hers, conveying unspoken understanding and love.

In the evening, the ship docked at Jorhat Nimatighat, providing them with a temporary resting place. Exhausted from the emotional journey, Oikoli and Andrice sought refuge in each other's arms, finding comfort in their shared love. Their dreams and aspirations for the future remained intact, interwoven with the memories they had left behind.

As they prepared for the night, Oikoli's heart carried a mix of longing and anticipation. The path ahead was uncertain, but she knew that with Andrice by her side, they would face whatever challenges awaited them. They embraced the bittersweet reality of their departure from Disangmukh, holding onto the belief that their love would serve as the guiding light through the uncharted waters of their future.

"Andrice, my compass in this vast ocean," she reflected, *"with you, the whispers of Disangmukh will guide us. Together, we shall navigate the tides of change, our love the beacon in the darkness."*

In the depths of their souls, Oikoli and Andrice carried the essence of Disangmukh, the whispers of the river, and the memories of their beloved village. As they closed their eyes that night, their dreams intertwined with the reality that lay ahead, painting a vivid picture of a life filled with love, resilience, and the courage to embrace new horizons.

The beginning is always today.

— Mary Shelley

CHAPTER

12

Love Tested

"Love is not love which alters when it alteration finds."

– William Shakespeare, Sonnet 116

"Love is an endless act of forgiveness. Forgiveness is the key to action and freedom." – Maya Angelou

The ship's cabin had become their sanctuary, a place where Oikoli and Andricerevelled in their newfound love. The air was thick with the scent of their passion, and the world outside seemed to fade away as they clung to each other. It was a love that transcended language, a love that needed no words to express its intensity.

Andrice, consumed by desire, couldn't bear to let Oikoli out of his sight. He held her in a fervent embrace, his kisses tasting of both longing and promise. The other members of the dockyard, understanding the depth of their connection, discreetly left them alone, giving the couple the privacy they desired.

In those moments, Andrice was intoxicated by Oikoli's presence. Her warmth, her wild rustic scent, and her innate elegance overwhelmed him. She was a world unto herself, a world he longed to explore with every kiss and touch. He was enraptured by the exotic allure of this village beauty who had stolen his heart.

Oikoli, in Andrice's arms, felt a sense of fulfillment she had never known before. His obsession with her was intoxicating, and she revelled in the attention he lavished upon her. In his embrace, she discovered a passion that ignited her very soul. Her heart beat in time with his, and the world outside seemed to cease to exist.

But as the days passed and the ship carried them away from Disangmukh, they encountered the harsh reality of their communication barrier. Oikoli, fluent in Misings and with a smattering of Assamese, found herself unable to converse with Andrice, who spoke only English. What had once seemed like a minor inconvenience now loomed as a significant obstacle in their relationship.

Love, for all its beauty, could not bridge the chasm of language that separated them. While their physical connection remained strong, they struggled to understand each other's desires and needs. Life was more than just kisses, cuddles, and hugs—it was about comprehending the depths of one another's hearts.

Oikoli, resourceful and determined, sought the help of Bengali Babu, their mutual confidant. Through gestures and a few words, she learned that Andrice would soon return to England. The realization hit her like a tidal wave. Andrice had been trying to convey his intention to take her to England, but the message had been lost in translation.

The truth hit Oikoli hard. She had married Andrice in a whirlwind of emotions, but she had not been prepared to leave Assam, her beloved DisangMorisuti, and the life she had known. The prospect of departing this place, so deeply rooted in her heart, filled her with trepidation.

One day, in Andrice's absence, as she organized their belongings, Oikoli stumbled upon a trace map hidden in a portable trace bag. She held the map, her fingers tracing the unfamiliar lines, and an idea took root. If she were to burn this trace map, perhaps Andrice would not be able to return to England.

Without hesitation, she set the trace map ablaze, watching as it turned to ashes. It was a desperate act, born out of love and fear, an attempt to keep Andrice with her in this land she cherished.

When Andrice returned and realized the tracemap was missing, he questioned Oikoli about it. He showed her his hand gesture, mimicking the act of sailing down and raising it high, trying to convey his intention of taking her to England. But all that remained of the trace map were ashes.

Oikoli couldn't comprehend Andrice's frustration and anger. She knew he was scolding her, but the words meant nothing to her. Alone in Andrice's absence, she wept silently, feeling the weight of her actions and the uncertainty of her future.

The night stretched on as Oikoli wrestled with uncertainty. She pondered whether Andrice's intentions were to take her to England or if she was merely an object of his desire. The future was a vast, uncharted territory.

> *"Will I return home? Who will assist me? What will become of me?" Oikoli was besieged by doubts, craving answers that eluded her.*

Awaiting Andrice's return, Oikoli felt her world coming undone. The certainty of her love now gave way to a future shrouded in doubt. She longed for DisangMorisuti, the familiarity of her past, and the man who had captured her heart.

Andrice, returning late and exhausted, refrained from waking Oikoli. Sensing a rift in their bond, he lay beside her in the dim cabin, contemplating the silent gulf that had formed between them.

Their love was now subjected to its greatest challenge, tested by cultural and linguistic barriers and unspoken expectations.

How long does their love story, woven from both joy and adversity, stand as a testament to the resilience of the human heart against the unknown?

Oikoli's internal struggle was palpable. She was torn between her love for Andrice and her connection to her homeland. ***"Will he take me to England, or am I just a fleeting desire?"*** she questioned herself in the silence of the night.

Andrice faced his own introspection, recognizing that his actions, though well-intentioned, had contributed to their current plight. He contemplated the essence of love amidst their cultural divide.

As life moved on around them, Andrice's determination to communicate his plans to Oikoli intensified. He desperately sought to convey his wish to start a new life with her in England.

Oikoli, however, remained conflicted, her heart split between her love for Andrice and her homeland. She realized that love alone couldn't simplify the complexities they faced. True understanding was needed beyond physical affection.

In solitude, Oikoli revisited the night she burned the tracemap, recalling Andrice's incomprehensible anger. The memory left her feeling isolated, adrift in a world she struggled to grasp.

As they navigated the early trials of marriage, their love stood as both their anchor and their greatest test. Unseen by the world, they waged silent battles within their hearts.

But In the midst of their trials, forgiveness would become their guiding light, paving the way for a future where love would truly know no bounds.

Epilogue

Time is the longest distance between two places

Tennessee Williams, **'The Glass Menagerie'**

As the sun sets on the poignant tale of Oikoli and AndriceBoklin, we find ourselves at the close of a chapter, but not the end of their story. The echoes of their love, a melody that once soared across the English skies, returned to the comforting embrace of India's vibrant hues. Siliguri became their sanctuary, a place where memories of their eldest son, like tender whispers of the past, nudged them away from England's shores.

In the heart of Siliguri, amidst the bustling streets and the serene vistas of the

Kanchenjunga, they sought solace. Yet, the winds of destiny, ever so fickle, whispered of England, a dream that lingered just beyond reach. They found themselves anchored in the warmth of Kolkata's embrace, the city's heartbeat syncing with their own.

Time, the silent weaver of fate, eventually guided them to Nimatighat Jorhat, where the roots of their love grew deep and wide, branching out as their family flourished. It was here, by the gentle flow of the Brahmaputra, that their saga continued, woven into the tapestry of life's intricate design.

In the historic town of Sivasagar, a woman of remarkable spirit traces her lineage to the storied past of Oikoli. She, the granddaughter of Oikoli, carries within her the whispers of the **Yein** clan from Disangmukh, each revelation a piece of the puzzle that is her heritage.

Their story, forever etched in the fabric of history, serves as a powerful reminder of love's lasting strength and our ability to persevere through life's challenges. As we close this chapter of their remarkable tale, we hold tight to the core of their life's tapestry—a rich heritage of love, interlaced with moments of sorrow, and a steadfast hope that illuminates our journey ahead.

"To love or have loved, that is enough. Ask nothing further. There is no other pearl to be found in the dark folds of life."

- Victor Hugo, 'Les Misérables'

Ode to My First Circle

To my Life's Companion, **Pompi Pegu** whose love has been the wind beneath the wings of my creativity, bringing a touch of romance to my writing that only the heart can know. She is the muse of my life's story, and her influence is woven through every word about love in these pages.

And to my colleagues—**Sanjay Das, Abhijit Borpujari, Mayashree Das, and Pooja Bhuyan**—who have been the perfect audience, lending their ears and sharing their perspectives as I navigated the waters of this novel. Their insights were like lighthouses guiding me to shore, ensuring that the narrative stayed true and the characters remained vibrant.

Their collective wisdom has not just enhanced this story but has also reminded me of the shared joy that comes from creating and storytelling.

Glossary of Mising Words

(Used Mising words and their meanings)

Karé Okum (TalengOkum/Ukum):

Traditional Mising house of raised stilt bamboo platform with Thatched roofs

Apong: Typically Rice beer of black and white variety. Both kampong Apong(white variety) and Po:roApong

ÉgAdín: Pork fleshrefers to both cooked and uncooked

Ya:mé Mímbír- Young boys and girls

Murong Okum/Ukum: Modern day club for the community. Traditional Mising Common house for the young boys and girls where villagers often sit for discussion or sometimes for feast and festival.

Ra:na:m: Boiled

Ba:na:m: Roasted

Pamnam: Baked

Ta:to - Ya:yo: Grandfather/mother (Grandparents)

KamponTani: White people or people with white complexion

Sédi Mélo: Mising people worship the entity that is integral to their worldview. Supreme heavenly power. Generally refers to the **Father** and **Mother** entity

Donyi: Po:lo: the Sun and the Moon.

Koneng: Mising Word for an Unmarried Girl

Ege Gasor: Mising Dress worn by Women

Meet the Author

SHIVA PRASAD MILI, the **Head of the Department of English**at Sibsagar Girls' College under Dibrugarh University, is a distinguished author and a key figure in promoting the cultural heritage of Disangmukh through his literary works. His notable publications include **"Beliefs Across the River: Chronicles of the Mising Villages," "Run: Drive for Movement and Purpose," "Grammar Made Easy: Fluency Fix for English Learners,""Essential Introduction to English Poetry: A Guide for GEC Students,"** and **"30 Must-Know Keys to Mastering Spoken English."** He has also edited **"English Language Teaching: North East Perspective."** These works are available on platforms like Amazon, Flipkart, Goodreads, and Notion Press in both ebook and paperback formats. In addition to his literary achievements, Mili serves as **the Secretary**cum **Convener** of the **English Language Teachers' Association of India, Upper Assam Chapter**, and has trained over 1000 teachers and students in English proficiency and spoken English. His contributions have significantly enriched the educational landscape, particularly in the field of English language teaching in Northeast India.